# THE CHRISTMAS MICE

# The Christmas Mice

by
John W. White

illustrated by
Dorothy Benson Torres

An Angelfood book
STILLPOINT PUBLISHING
WALPOLE, NEW HAMPSHIRE

This book is manufactured in the United States of America. It is designed by James F. Brisson, cover art by Dorothy Benson Torres and published by Stillpoint Publishing, Box 640, Meetinghouse Road, Walpole, NH 03608. Published simultaneously in Canada by Fitzhenry & Whiteside Limited, Toronto.

Library of Congress Catalog Card Number: 84-50927

ISBN 0-913299-15-4

0 9 8 7 6 5 4 3 2 1

*With love to:*

*Sandy, Tucker, Sharon and Timmy*
*Jason and Candy*
*Sherry*
*William*
*and to their children*
*and their children's children*
*through the years.*

Roger felt very sad. He couldn't help it that when he was born he was different from the other mice. They were brown but he was green!

Some of the mice teased him about it. That wasn't nice, of course. But they weren't nicemice — they were meanmice. Whenever they saw Roger, they laughed and chased him and called him names. "Oh Roger!" they would say in mousetalk. "You're not brown like us. You're green and you look so silly!"

Poor Roger! No one would play with him. It seemed as if the whole mousetown didn't like him. So he ran away and hid in the forest at the edge of the meadow where he felt he wouldn't be seen. Then he would watch the meadowmice while they played, wishing he could do something so they would like him. He thought and thought, but he just couldn't think of anything to make the brown mice his friends.

It was a lonely summer for Roger. Then one day, a very strange thing happened. He heard an awful squeak, followed by a crash. When he ran to see what it was, out of the bushes walked a *red* mouse!

"Oh, my goodness!" squeaked Roger. "You're a red mouse. What happened to you?"

The red mouse said, "A hawk almost ate me. I was at the edge of the forest on the other side of the meadow, watching the mice play. All of a sudden, the hawk flew down and caught me. But I fought hard and got away. I'm sure lucky I landed in those bushes."

"You certainly are," said Roger. "Are you hurt?"

"No, I'm okay," the red mouse said, straightening its fur. Then it asked, "What's your name?"

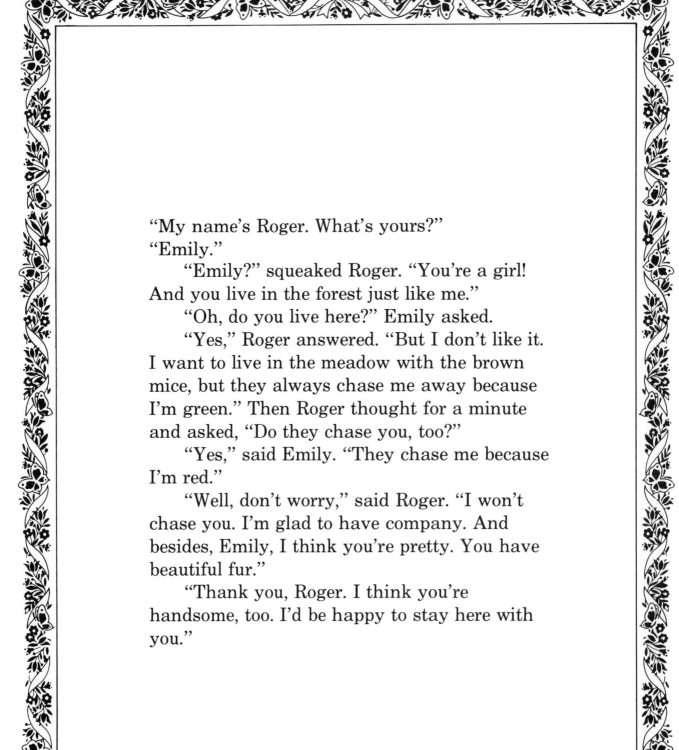

"My name's Roger. What's yours?"

"Emily."

"Emily?" squeaked Roger. "You're a girl! And you live in the forest just like me."

"Oh, do you live here?" Emily asked.

"Yes," Roger answered. "But I don't like it. I want to live in the meadow with the brown mice, but they always chase me away because I'm green." Then Roger thought for a minute and asked, "Do they chase you, too?"

"Yes," said Emily. "They chase me because I'm red."

"Well, don't worry," said Roger. "I won't chase you. I'm glad to have company. And besides, Emily, I think you're pretty. You have beautiful fur."

"Thank you, Roger. I think you're handsome, too. I'd be happy to stay here with you."

So Roger and Emily were mousemarried. They lived in Roger's nest among the roots of a tall oak tree and were companions for each other. They fixed up their mousehouse with pretty leaves, and they didn't even think of the meadowmice in the mousetown. They just played all day in the forest. Sometimes, though, they were puzzled to hear sounds from the meadow, as if the mice were fighting among themselves.

Summer ended and the weather began to get cold. One day Emily said, "Roger, I have a surprise. Guess what? We're going to have babies."

When Roger heard that, he felt so happy that he jumped up and ran out of the nest, right into the meadow. He didn't even think of what had happened when he had lived there. He was just so happy that he wanted to share it with everyone. So he ran and ran, shouting, "We're going to have babies! We're going to have babies!"

The meadowmice were so surprised when Roger ran by that they didn't try to tease him or chase him. They just looked at each other and wondered about his strange behavior. One of them — an elder mouse — said, "Do you think Roger went crazy because he was all alone? Maybe we were too mean to him. Things haven't seemed so good since we drove him away."

But Roger wasn't crazy — he was just happy, deliriously happy. So he kept on running all the way back to his nest, and when he got there he gave Emily a nice whiskerkiss.

The winter arrived and snow fell. Emily said the babies would be born soon, so Roger stayed at home with her except to go out for food. One evening Roger went to find dinner. He hopped and scurried through the snow until he came to the edge of the forest. In the middle of the meadow next to the mousetown, he saw something that made him stop and look. It was a beautiful tree, shining with lights and tinsel and pretty bulbs. Roger thought he had never seen anything so lovely.

All the meadowmice were gathered around the tree, gazing at it. They didn't notice Roger approach. An elder mouse said, "I saw people putting it here. I guess it must be for us. I wonder why they did it?"

Roger heard the question. He thought of Emily and the babies, and he thought of them eventually being teased and chased by the meadowmice. When he thought of that, Roger decided he had to speak up and answer the question. He felt afraid, but he wanted his family to have a happy life, without fighting and trouble. So he took a deep breath and said, "I think I know why."

The meadowmice turned around in surprise and looked at Roger. His heart was beating fast because he expected them to be mean as they always were. But this time they just looked at Roger quietly. The lights of the pretty tree shone above them peacefully. So Roger took another deep breath and said, "I think they put the tree here to tell us that we ought to live without fighting and being mean. At least, that's the way I'd like it to be."

When Roger said that, the mice remembered the way they used to tease Roger and chase him and call him names. They remembered the way Roger used to watch them from the forest, with a sad look. And as they remembered it all, they felt ashamed and hung their heads.

Then the elder mouse who had asked the question looked at Roger and said, "Roger, you're right. We shouldn't have been so mean. Since we drove you away, it seems we haven't gotten along so well in the mousetown. I'm sorry, Roger. Will you be my friend?"

"Yes, Roger," said another. "I'm sorry, too. Please don't be sad any more. I'm ashamed of being so mean to you."

Then the other mice said they were really sorry, too. Roger could hardly believe it! He had been alone in the forest for so long, trying to think of how to make the mice like him. But he never could. Then when Emily showed up, he was so happy that he forgot to think about it.

And now, without his even trying, the mice were being friendly just because he had been brave. By being brave, he had made the brown mice see how wrong they were to be mean. And that changed them from meanmice to nicemice.

"Come on, Roger," a mouse shouted. "Let's play tag. You're it!" Soon Roger was running around the meadow with the brown mice, laughing and playing like he had always wanted. He was having a wonderful time. And the meadowmice were too, now that they were together once more.

Suddenly Roger remembered Emily. "Oh, my goodness!" he squeaked. "I forgot about Emily. I've got to go home to see if the babies are here yet."

"What babies, Roger?" asked the mice. But there was no answer because Roger was scampering home through the twilight.

"What a strange way to act," said a mouse. "It's just like the day he ran through here shouting about babies. I wonder who Emily is?"

Then another mouse said, "I remember Emily. She's the red mouse who got caught by the hawk. Remember that day we saw her fighting with him in the sky? She fell into the forest where Roger lives."

Then the mice started wondering if Roger really did mean what he said about babies. "Do you suppose Emily wasn't killed?" one said. Another said, "What if Roger met her and they got married? Maybe Emily is his wife. Maybe she's going to have babies soon. Come on. Let's go see."

But by then it was too dark to see, so they decided to meet by the pretty tree in the morning.

The next day, all the mice came squeaking and chattering through the snow. As they hopped along, one mouse said, "Roger wouldn't lie to us. I bet there really are babies. I wonder what color they'll be?"

When they got to the forest, they called, "Roger, where are you?" Soon Roger hopped out. He seemed very happy and excited, but he just put his paw up and went "shhh" so the

mice would be quiet. Then he said, "Listen, everyone. I want you to be quiet because the babies are sleeping."

The mice looked at each other and nodded their heads. "See?" said the mouse who had spoken before. "I told you he wasn't fooling. There really are babies. Tell us about them, Roger. Can we see them?"

"Sure," said Roger. "There are two boys and two girls. They were born last night and their mother is Emily. I met her last summer after she got away from a hawk. You used to tease her, too, because her fur is red. But when we met, we were so happy that we forgot about you. Now the babies are here and we love them so much. Come in and see them."

So the meadowmice started in, one by one, to look at the babies. But as soon as the first mouse saw them, he ran back to the door and whispered, "They're brown — just like us!"

The other mice were amazed. How could a red mouse and a green mouse have babies that were brown? None of them could explain it.

They didn't know that red and green make brown, just like when red and green paint are mixed. Roger and Emily didn't know that either, but they wouldn't have cared anyway. They were just very pleased to have four nice babies.

Roger and Emily stood side by side, watching proudly as the meadowmice looked at their babies. Then an elder mouse entered. It was the one who first talked to Roger by the pretty tree. When he came in, he started to look at the babies, but then he stopped. He looked at Roger and Emily, thought a while, and then said, "Listen, everyone. I just remembered something. Yesterday I heard people talking by the pretty tree, and they said that today is Christmas. So that tree in the meadow must be a Christmas tree. Or maybe I should say it's a Christmouse tree."

He paused for a moment. All the mice were quiet, listening to him, so he continued speaking. He asked, "Did you know there are special colors for Christmas? Well, there are.

I heard people say it. The colors are red and green — the same as Roger and Emily. They're the colors of Christmas. They must be Christmas mice."

The meadowmice were puzzled. What did the elder mouse mean? They looked at Roger and Emily and the babies. Roger was green and Emily was red — not at all like the meadowmice. And yet what pretty babies they had — brown, just like the meadowmice. It was very strange.

"Don't you understand?" asked the elder mouse. "Look at them and look at the babies. See? The color of their fur doesn't matter. They're still mice, like us. And the babies prove it. They're beautiful, aren't they?"

Slowly the mice understood what the elder mouse was saying — that it was wrong for them to be mean to Roger and Emily just because their fur was a different color. Being mean had upset the mousetown too, so it had hurt everyone. The mice were quiet, thinking about what the elder mouse had said.

Just then, the babies started waking up. Roger said, "Come on, Emily. Let's take them outside so they can see what the world is like."

He picked up two of the babies and went outside. Emily followed with the other two. When they stepped into the sunlight, the elder mouse shouted, "Let's give three cheers for Roger and Emily, the Christmas mice. Hip, hip, hooray!" All the other mice cheered, squeaking as loud as their little voices could. Roger and Emily stood together quietly, looking very pleased. Roger thought, "Now I'm sure our babies won't be treated badly the way we were. What a wonderful day this is!"

He held up the babies and said to them, "See, little babies. See what a nice place the world is."

"When there's no fighting and being mean," said the elder mouse.

"You're right," said Roger. "Fighting and being mean are no good for us. Everything is so peaceful and nice today. I hope it stays this way all the time. In fact, I wish it was Christmas every day."

"So do I," said a mouse who had just scampered up to the group. "Because I was just at the Christmas tree, and guess what? There's food all around it. Come on."

It was true. All around the tree, food was scattered on the snow. There was cheese, there were crackers, there were sunflower seeds and nuts and every kind of food that animals like to eat. The humans had put it there while the mice were at Roger's nest. When the mice saw all the delicious things, they had a feast, stuffing in food until their cheeks were puffed up and their tummies were sticking out.

And when the last sunflower seed and the last nut were gone, the mice played games and talked and had lots of fun just being friendly with each other. And the ones who enjoyed it most were Roger and Emily, the Christmas mice. They fed little bits of cheese and crackers to the babies and held them up to watch the other mice running around playing. It was a lovely celebration for the entire mousetown.

"Oh, Roger," said Emily. "This is so wonderful. I'm glad we're friends with the mice now."

"Me too," said Roger. "And you know what? It's because of the babies. That's how we became friends — because of the babies. Isn't that strange? It took some babies to teach grown-ups to be nice to each other. Do you suppose that has anything to do with Christmas?"

The elder mouse was nearby, and when he heard Roger say that, he just smiled to himself. He remembered hearing the humans talking, so he knew about the baby who came on the first Christmas to stop people from fighting and being mean. But the elder mouse didn't say anything. He just smiled to himself because he knew the meaning of Christmas, and he knew that Roger was right.

So the elder mouse was silent and the meadowmice kept on playing, and Roger and Emily thought of building a nest in the meadow when spring came. And everyone was very, very happy.